Sugar Blue

LOTHROP BOOKS BY
VERA AND BILL CLEAVER

The Kissimmee Kid
A Little Destiny

ALSO BY VERA AND BILL CLEAVER

Delpha Green & Company
Dust of the Earth
Ellen Grae
Grover
Hazel Rye
I Would Rather Be a Turnip
Lady Ellen Grae
Me Too
The Mimosa Tree
The Mock Revolt
Queen of Hearts
Trial Valley
Where the Lilies Bloom
The Whys and Wherefores of Littabelle Lee

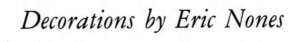

Decorations by Eric Nones

VERA CLEAVER

Sugar Blue

Lothrop, Lee & Shepard Books

NEW YORK

2   3   4   5   6   7   8   9   10

Library of Congress Cataloging in Publication Data

Cleaver, Vera.
Sugar Blue.

Summary: Distinctly unenthusiastic when her four-year-old niece, Ella, comes
for a prolonged visit, eleven-year-old Amy finds her increasingly close
relationship with the small girl gradually changing her view of herself and life
in general.
[1. Family life—Fiction] I. Title.
PZ7.C57926Su 1984   [Fic]   83-19910
ISBN 0-688-02720-2

Design by Lynn Braswell

15045

Sugar Blue

One

THIS WAS THE TIME of Amy Blue and this was her place, this hillside town in the southern sun named Myrtle Park where, in the warmed afternoons, sailboats put out from the shores of the surrounding lakes. In the evenings frogs stuttered their vespers in the street trees, one of which shaded the entranceway to The Cupboard Door, a catering service operated by Amy Blue's parents.

Amy had fox-bright eyes and, having lived eleven years, she had tamed most of her old, early terrors. Now, no claws waited in the dark to grab her. The black shape behind the washing machine in the basement was not an escaped maniac, but a trunk filled with quilts and blankets. The doctor did not draw blood from her because he was a blood fiend and thirsted for it, but because under his microscope her blood told him things.

"What things? What have I got?" croaked Amy. A conniving child, full of fuss and self, she set a scheming eye on the doctor.

The doctor was a battered old veteran who knew how to deal with a faker. He simply took charge of the situation. He wanted to know where in her body there was hurt when she had one of her heart-stopping spells.

"Oh, everywhere," groaned Amy. "Grrrrr. It feels like horses in my head. And I turn white all over."

"Do you look?" inquired the doctor.

"Yes, sir," prattled Amy. "I always look. But what color I am when my heart stops doesn't make any difference. I don't care. I just care about what makes it quit."

The doctor wondered why nobody else had ever witnessed one of her seizures. He said there wasn't a thing wrong with her heart, that he wished his was as strong and healthy as hers. He said that she had nice blood, a nice texture and all, and that it had been a pleasure for him to examine it. He patted her mother's hand and said, "Courage, Marie."

To Amy neither her mother nor father were now the awesome miracles they once had been. Their old wonderful powers and ways were gone. They had no time now to sing or laugh. They were a pair of machines, and it was fascinating to see how they made their wheels spin. How they spun when the grandparents were expected! The grandparents' name was Harney, and those two old soured ones loved to come for visits. Bristling with opinions and authority and jealous suspicions, they came to sniff and pry, to gaze upon what had once been theirs: the old proud house with the shimmering bed of Myrtle Lake at its front door, their daughter Marie Blue, and The Cupboard Door.

Huffing and puffing their disapproval, the grandparents moved furniture around to their liking. They dug out the new rose hedge and replaced the bushes with some they said were more sensible. In the room where they slept and passed their leisure hours, they talked loud and long. Their talk floated down, filling the dark twist of the stairwell.

Their talk filled Amy's quick young ears, and she took refuge in her own room. There were no voices there save her own and the one that spoke to her from her mirror, the voice of Image.

Standing before the mirror, Amy put ribbon bows in her hair and, breathing delicately, leaned to her image, liking the sheen of its smile, the graceful line of its neck, the way the little red hair tendrils curled about its cheeks.

"Nice," said Amy. "You're so nice. So sweet and pretty. I like you. Do you like me? Just a little?"

"I like you a whole lot," asserted Image.

"Not many do," said Amy.

Image cast a sly look. "Do you care?"

"No. Not much. Not any. I don't care."

"Then why are we talking about it?"

"I don't know," said Amy, and rested her chin in her hand. "It must be because I remember things. I don't like to remember, do you?"

"No," said Image. "It makes me feel grrrrr."

"But some days what I don't want to remember won't go away."

Sympathetically Image smiled. It understood.

"I don't like people," said Amy.

"They're pills," responded Image.

"I keep remembering how it used to be before we came here to live," said Amy. "Do you remember that? Our house trailer?"

"Down by the ocean," said Image.

"I liked to look at the ocean," said Amy.

"So did I," said Image.

"So did Dad. Mama too," said Amy. "Now they don't like anything. I don't think they even like me very much."

"They don't like themselves," commented Image.

"They like to collect money," said Amy. "Whrrrrr. Make the adding machine go. Count the money. Run to the bank. Run back. Bake the cakes. Make the salads. Don't forget the onions. Chop, chop."

Image yawned.

Asked Amy, "Do you remember Dad's shrimp boat?"

"Another boat ran into it and it sank," said Image. "And then the people from the bank took the house trailer away and Grandpa Harney said we had to come here to live."

Amy put another ribbon bow in her hair. Beyond the windows in her room the world was green and yellow and alive. It rustled and spoke knowingly of life and yet for all it knew of Amy she might just as well have been a pebble or a termite. After all, who was she, this girl who held herself so apart from others? And of what was she made, this one who closed her eyes to the world? Her confidence was so absurd. She herself was absurd, she and all of her little cupcake vanities.

Amy made her eyes big and pinched her cheeks to make them blush with color, while down on the Blues' wide plain of beach and across their lawns the wind bellowed a March ruckus. And in their room the grandparents sipped their coffee and spoke their criticisms of Amy and her father.

But now it was early June and it was not the grandparents who had come. To this reality Amy opened her eyes one irritable morning and looked up into those of her father. Her father's eyes were brown and had little tunnels in them that led to—well, where did they lead? To where her father hid himself? Where was that? And what did he do there? Play again in the ocean? Help her mother build a sand castle? Eat hot dogs? Sleep under the umbrella? Watch the moon come up? Old moon. Old creepy questions. No answers to them. It had crossed Amy's mind more than once that this man with brown eyes was not her real father, that her real father might have drowned the day his shrimp boat was destroyed

14

and that he had sent this other person to take his place.

Amy closed her eyes and opened them again. This time they took in the whole of her father and the little girl clinging to his hand.

Eyeing the child, Amy sat up. "What," she asked, "is that?"

Her father's look was neatly arranged. "This is Ella, Mildred's little girl." He brought the child around to stand in front of him and without any show of anything bent to her. "Say hello to Amy, Ella."

"Hello," piped Ella. Her smile was a song. "Hello. I got to ride in the airplane and the lady gave me a peach and some soup."

Amy swung her legs over the side of the bed and set her feet on the floor. Her hair was in her eyes, and she peered out through the strands of it. "That's my sister's kid? She can't be. Mildred's kid is just a little baby."

"She was a baby the last time you saw her two years ago," said Tom Blue. "Now she's four years old. She's this little girl." An expression of strain had come over his face, and he asked, "Are you awake, Amy?"

Still with her eyes clamped on Ella, Amy sat in the stiff, hunched attitude of an old suspicious woman. "I don't know. Give me a minute."

"One minute," said her father.

"If that's Mildred's kid then I'm her aunt," said Amy.

"Yes," said her father. "You're her aunt."

Said Amy, "What I want to know is, what's she doing here? She doesn't belong here. She belongs to be with Mildred in North Carolina." Discovering a thought she tugged at the pants to her pajamas and set her elbows on her bare knees. They were milk white and marked only by a couple of little scars left over from her days of living by the ocean—those lovely, different days before The Cupboard Door and the big house had entered her life. Then The Cupboard Door had belonged to Grandpa and Grandma Harney. They had lived in the house, and visits to them had been a little on the strained side. They had never said so, but children made them nervous, a fact first noticed by Mildred. When Grandpa and Grandma Harney left Myrtle Park to go to Georgia to live, Mildred said she hoped that none of their farm neighbors had any kids.

Mildred. The thought of her jabbed again at Amy, and she stood, allowing the legs to her pajama pants to fall down around her ankles. "Mildred," she said. "Mildred's home. After all this time she's decided to stop writing all those stingy letters and pay us a visit."

16

"The airplane was cold and the lady that took care of me covered me up with a blanket," said Ella, making a gentle offering. Squirming away from Tom Blue's hand, she skipped to the windows and knelt at a sill, looking out. "Oh, how pretty!" she exclaimed.

"Mildred has not come home," stated Amy's father. "After you went to bed last night she phoned to ask if it would be convenient for us to have Ella stay with us for a while, and we said it would be. Can you pull yourself together, Amy? I'll explain what's going on if you can pull yourself together, but I don't want to have to go through it twice. Your mother and I have a wedding to cater today, and I'm in a hurry. It took me an hour and half to go to the airport and back. Are you awake now, Amy?"

"I'm together," said Amy. "I'm awake." She was only half awake. To get her blood going she stamped her feet and wagged her head from side to side. "I just barely remember what Mildred looks like. If it wasn't for her pictures I wouldn't remember at all. Did she bring her husband with her? How long are they going to stay? If they stay too long Grandpa Harney won't like it if he and Grandma come. He'll have one of his grrrrr fits. He hates kids. So does Grandma."

"Your grandpa," said Tom Blue, "is in no position right now to have a grrrrr fit over anything. He fell off a ladder yesterday and broke his knee, so your grandma put him in a hospital. Will you please stop that? What are you doing?"

"I'm waking up," replied Amy, and sat on the edge of her bed. The news that her grandfather lay in a hospital in his part of Georgia was like an itch that couldn't be reached. She thought that she should be sorry and say that she was, yet the words would not come. It would do her grandfather good to have to stay in bed and rest himself. He could listen to his radio and think about how to make his peaches and pecans grow bigger so when he sold them he'd make more money and wouldn't have to leave his farm and go off to the poorhouse or sleep under a tree. Her grandmother would take the place apart seeing to it that he had everything he wanted. Both of her grandparents had mean cases of the I Wants. They would shake their fists at the doctor. They knew how to scare people and get things done.

Still at the windows, still entranced with the outside scene, Ella had her hands in the air and was making the graceful motions of a bird in flight. She was dressed all in white and, with an ugly little shock, Amy realized that she was the most beautiful human being she had ever seen. A noise formed in Amy's throat. She swallowed it and swung her gaze to her father.

"Listen," he said. "Listen to me. Mildred is divorced from her husband."

Amy almost laughed. From her grandfather and her grandmother she knew all about divorce. There had never been one in either of their families and there was never going to be. Divorce was wicked. It was a sin. When you got married it was supposed to be forever. Only low-down, no-account, trashy people got divorced.

"Mildred can't be divorced," said Amy. "Grandpa wouldn't let her."

"She's been divorced for months," said her father. "She has a job and an apartment, and Ella has been going to day-care school, but the woman who runs it is sick now and has had to close it. Mildred needs time to find a new place for Ella to stay while she works, so she's going to live here with us for a while."

"Why," asked Amy, "didn't Mildred let us know about her divorce before?"

"Your sister is young and has a mind of her own," answered Tom Blue. Emphatically, his voice rose. "Ella will sleep in here with you. This room is big and pleasant. Nice wide bed."

"It's not as wide as it looks," said Amy.

"If you share this room we won't have to go to the expense of buying another air-conditioning unit," reasoned her father. "And we'll save on electricity too."

"Are you going to leave her here with me while you go off to do your wedding?" asked Amy.

"That's the idea," answered her father. "A little responsibility won't kill you."

"She'll want me to play house," warned Amy, unable to think of anything more formidable. "What will I do with her besides that? I haven't played house in a hundred years. I forgot how."

"Put your mind to it and you'll remember," said her father. "Take her around the neighborhood and show her where everybody lives. Entertain her. If all I had to do was entertain one little girl I wouldn't have any trouble." He went out into the hallway and returned with three pieces of green luggage. "Her clothes are in here. Your mother will unpack them when we get home this evening. Any more questions?"

Amy shook her head. Questions evaded her. She felt as she had felt that time she had dived into Lake Myrtle. She would have draped herself over a burning bush for five days to have been able to leave the springboard with a clean leap and to have this followed by the applause of an audience. The Blues did not have a springboard, so she used the one that belonged to the nearest neighbors, winter residents who kept their house closed during the summers. And there had been no audience.

The dive had been a belly buster. She had hit the water flat, and its little demon waves had danced toward her, closed around her, held her in a slippery, suffocating grip. To free herself and dog paddle back to safety had been a confused triumph and one without a glow. She still remembered the confusion, the awful sense of aloneness, the feeling of being managed by some rude and interfering force.

Remembering all of this, Amy shook herself like a wet dog and turned her attention to Ella. Amy knew little of children smaller than herself, but what she knew was enough. Those who hadn't yet learned how to talk knew things nobody else did. The way they slunked their eyes around and the way they laughed at nothing was creepy. Those who had learned how to talk didn't know enough to come in out of a shower of mud. They believed everything and they would do anything. You could tell them that you needed a brick stretcher or a cloud hook and they would trot off and try to get it for you. If they thought of it they would jump off a cliff just to see if there was water under it. The people who had lived in the only

21

house on Lake Myrtle Drive that sported a red door and a red chimney had had kids like that: one who talked and one who didn't. Now a couple of old ones had the place, but its front door was still a brilliant red and so was its chimney.

Today the occupants of this house were not in their usual terrace chairs. Showing Ella around the neighborhood, Amy took note of this, saying, "They must be out back, else they'd be in their chairs. It's not raining."

"No," agreed Ella, "it's not raining."

I could tell her it was and she'd say she felt a drop, thought Amy. "Look at that door and that chimney," she said. "Stand still a minute and look. Somebody should tell the people who live there to either paint their door and chimney a different color or get out of town. Look at that mess. When I look at it I think I'm a fool-crazy. What does it make you think of?"

"Santa Claus," decided Ella, so golden, so full of smile. "And snow. When does it snow here?"

Jolted, Amy felt a quiver in her jaw. Long ago she had learned that snow in her part of Florida was a Large Event. She had never seen snow, but once, as a Christmas had approached, her grandfather had proven to her that there was no Santa Claus, that he was only a man doing a job. On this particular Christmas the Blues were guests at the big house on Lake Myrtle Drive, and one morning Grandpa Harney took Amy to town with him. She thought it was going to be a trip just for fun, but it was not.

Her department store Santa Claus had had a left forefinger that crooked to one side, which appeared to be the result of some old injury. With a sly old eye Grandfather had pointed the finger out to her, first in the store and then again later on in the diner across the street, where Santa, in street clothes, sat sipping his coffee and reading his evening paper. Santa was, said Grandfather, a big lie and so were his reindeer. Reindeer couldn't fly. If they could there wouldn't have been any use for the airplane to have been invented. People would just stake out a few reindeer on their roofs and when they got ready to take a trip they'd hook the animals up to a sleigh and take off. Only idiots, said Grandfather, believed in Santa Claus and his reindeer. Was Amy an idiot?

Amy had decided that she was not. Not if believing in Santa meant that she was one.

But now here was this kid still believing there was a Santa Claus. Probably she believed in a lot of other idiot baby things too. She'd want to talk about them. There wouldn't be any talk with her that would make any sense. There wouldn't be any getting away from her either, not even at night. Probably she'd hog the whole bed.

The couple who owned the house with the red door and the red chimney came out of their side door and seated themselves on their terrace. Under a high sky Myrtle Lake lay calm and, without any formed purpose in mind, Amy said, "I can't say for sure when it snows here. Sometimes it does when it's hot, like now. You know what a brick stretcher is?"

Ella considered. "No."

"It's a little do-flingy that stretches bricks," said Amy. "I'm going to get one pretty soon. That way when I'm building something and run out of bricks all I'll have to do is use my stretcher."

"What color is it going to be?" asked Ella.

"The one I'm going to get is orange, but they come in all colors," answered Amy. "I'm going to get my dad a pink one for Christmas." She blew a breath into her fist. "Everything's different here than it is where you've been. Christmas and Santa Claus don't come at their regular time. Nobody knows when they'll come. What you have to do is watch out for them."

A faraway look tiptoed across Ella's shining face. "We always put out stuff to eat for Santa when he gets to our house. Cookies. Little ones. Mama makes them and I help her."

24

"Here," said Amy, "we don't fool around with cookies for Santa. If he's hungry he goes to Sally's Diner to eat. Come on, you've seen the whole neighborhood. We'll go down on our beach for a while. We can't go near the water because there aren't any grownups around, but we can look at whatever else is down there. I'll let you go first because there might be a snake."

"A snake," said Ella, and covered her laughter with a hand. On the beach she discovered snail shells and gathered empty ones discarded by birds. Fascinated with these, loving them, she squatted in the sand, turning them this way and that to examine their colors and shapes. "They're sweet. Aren't they sweet?"

"They're shells," said Amy. The wind had come up and was moving across the lake, wrinkling its surface, and in the distance there was the sound of a truck in motion.

"I hear a truck," said Ella. "My daddy drives a truck." Still squatting, she twisted around and, in an attitude of listening, cocked her head. She put her teeth in her lip and held her hands as if they needed comforting. Something in the lake made a splash, and the sound of the truck faded. Ella again busied herself with the snail shells.

Seated on a patch of clean, dry grass, Amy watched her new responsibility and searched her mind for something good to think about, but her thoughts were only mutterings. What with this kid hanging on to her every word and her every step, how could things be anything but bad? She was going to have to share her room, her closet, even the air she breathed with somebody she didn't even know. The kid was pure. With a face like that she had to be, so there would be no more of lounging around in Grandmother and Grandfather's room during the long, sweet afternoons. The room was off limits to her, but she had never harmed it and had never taken anything from it. When it was raining or when it was cold she did take the china pot and one of the little fluted cups from their cabinet and did brew a cup or two of the special coffee. And once in a while she did take the tin box from its hiding place and help herself to one of Grandma Harney's chocolate candies, but she wasn't a criminal. The dab of coffee she used was never missed and it wasn't as though the candy was anything valuable.

Whenever she happened to think of them she prayed to be delivered of her sins. This didn't take long because she was not guilty of many. Amy did not regard vanity as a sin.

In the sand Ella had constructed a snail shell necklace and was pleased with it. "My mama's got a real one that looks something like this. It's not made out of shells though. My daddy gave it to her."

"Well," said Amy, "I guess that's better than having somebody give you a sharp stick in the eye. It's been so long since I last saw your daddy I don't remember him much. What does he look like?"

Ella ducked her head. "Big."

"What else?"

"He's got a lot of hair."

"Just on his head or does he grow it on his face too?" asked Amy. She hadn't the remotest interest in this detail and only inquired after it for lack of something else to say.

"He grows it on his face too," said Ella, rearranging the shell necklace.

"The man who comes to read our electric meter has got enough hair on his face to make me a fur coat," commented Amy. There wasn't a shred of truth in this remark, but she thought it was the most clever one she had ever thought of.

Under her breath Ella began to hum, and the faint, roving sound of this pricked at Amy's nerves. Why was it that little kids always had to make noise and why was it their hands always had to be pulling and pawing at something? Because they had mush in their heads where their brains belonged, that was why. No wonder their daddies and mamas dumped them, got rid of them, pushed them off onto somebody else to take care of.

Again, way out in the lake, there was a leaping and splashing commotion, and within Amy restlessness stirred. Playing with this feeling, goading it, she set her gaze on Ella. "How come your mama and daddy got divorced?"

Ella looked up. "I don't know."

"That's not very smart," said Amy. "Your mama and daddy got a divorce and you don't know why."

"It wasn't on account of Brad," said Ella. "We didn't know him till we went to live in our apartment."

"Who," inquired Amy, "is Brad?"

"His other name is Holt," explained Ella. "He's the one that takes the snow away when it comes so people won't fall down in it and when our windows get stuck he fixes them. He's got a car and when we go to the park Mama drives it. I get to ride the pony. Brad doesn't let me fall off."

"Brad takes the snow away so what people won't fall down in it?" asked Amy.

"The people who live where our apartment is," answered Ella. "In the same house."

"Does Brad live there too?"

"Yes."

"Who with?"

"By himself."

Disappointed, Amy looked at the sky. It was brilliantly clear and brilliantly honest. It would have been interesting to hear that Brad lived with a goat or a lunatic, but here he was, old, common Brad grubbing it out all by himself in his little grubby apartment. His car was the grandfather kind. It was black and he washed it every Saturday. Each morning for his breakfast he ate shredded wheat with hot water poured over it and the park was the only place he ever went because it didn't cost anything to get in. Brad wasn't manly, Amy decided. He could fix stuck windows and take the snow away, but his feet were little, like a woman's, and he had to wear suspenders to keep his pants from falling down. He had a round, country face.

Satisfied with her mental picture of Brad, Amy said, "We didn't finish talking about your daddy. How come you didn't go to live with him when he and your mama got a divorce?"

Clean and pink, Ella's tongue came out of her mouth and ran around her lips. "He said he didn't want me."

"He said that?" cried Amy. "Well, I don't know why. Most any fool would want you!" Unmoving and unmoved, in a more relaxed tone, she said, "What did you do when he told you that?"

"I put some oysters in his bed," said Ella.

As if something or someone had jerked her so, Amy sat erect. "Raw ones or cooked ones?"

"I got them out of a can," said Ella. "They were cold."

"Aha!" exclaimed Amy. "Ha. That's funny. Was it dark when you put them in his bed?"

"Sort of," said Ella.

"Then what happened? What did your daddy do?"

"Screamed. Jumped out. Knocked the lamp over. It broke so he couldn't see."

"Where were you?"

"In my room. I fixed the door so I could watch him."

"If it was dark," reasoned Amy, "he must have thought the oysters were something else. What did he do after he knocked the lamp over?"

"Screamed some more. Hollered for Mama to come quick and bring a knife but she didn't," said Ella and, in a sudden little frenzy, sprang to her feet and galloped around, first in a small circle and then in a widening one, tossing her head and snorting, pretending to be a horse. When she came back to her shells she was panting and said that she needed a drink of water.

She drank so much water that day that Amy felt called upon to report this to her parents when they came from work. They questioned and she told them that she and Ella had only eaten from the covered dishes in the refrigerator and had drunk only water and milk.

Her father went for the fever thermometer, took Ella's temperature, and said that it was normal. He said her thirst was probably caused by all of the excitement in her day.

The Blues and Ella ate their evening meal on the screened side patio, and afterward, while Amy and her father rinsed and put the dishes in the dishwasher, Amy's mother and Ella went upstairs to unpack Ella's clothing. In the lush, watered grasses down on the Blues' lakefront the insects were mostly quiet.

Those June days were full of Ella, and they were a little cruel to Amy. There was no more of lying abed with her head buried in her pillow to shut out the sounds of morning. With the first streak of daylight and the first bird chirp, Ella was instantly awake and instantly ready for anything. Rushing to meet the day, she bounced from bed to closet and from closet to bureau. "What dress do you want me to wear today? What did Grandma Blue do with my pink socks? Will you comb my hair? Wait, I haven't brushed my teeth yet. I think I had better take a bath. Mama always makes me. There. I'm clean but I've got soap in my ear. Will you get it out? Whew! Whew! That didn't feel good. What are we going to have for breakfast? What are we going to do today? Have Grandma and Grandpa already gone to work? Listen. What's that noise? Did you hear it? Who made it?"

"Nobody," said Amy and swallowed the tail end of her groan. The heavy southern heat had never bothered her much, but now it sucked at all of her strength and she became a clock watcher. It was only in the evenings when her parents were home that she felt free of Ella.

Nights with Ella were not funny. She had to be buttoned into her pajamas, had to have her hair brushed, had to look out at the fat moon and the stars, and had to talk. She said that her mama had told her that stars were the windows of heaven and sighed when Amy said that they weren't any such thing, that they were nothing but rocks rolling around in space. Unable to explain why they twinkled and what made them shine, Amy said, "They've got stuff on them, paint or something like that. Get in bed. We're supposed to sleep now."

"I think it's going to snow pretty soon," Ella

said, thumping her pillow. She put one leg in the air and said that as soon as it fell down she would be asleep, and this happened.

On the side of the bed she had staked out as hers, Amy composed herself for her own sleep. Usually this came as a quick whack to her head, but tonight it kept slipping away from her. Mildred and her divorced, truck driver husband came to sit in her mind and, though her memory of them was sketchy, she saw them clearly. They were like two actors on a stage. Mildred had her accordion strapped around her neck and was playing it, making it sound like she had lost something and was looking for it. Her husband held a big platter and gazed at the food heaped on it as though he might be waiting to hear the crack of a starting gun and hear somebody holler "Go." He didn't like Mildred's music.

There was white moonlight at the windows. The air conditioner hummed. There were footsteps and conversation on the stairway. A door closed. The figures on Amy's mind-stage faded. Sleep overtook her.

Several hours later she was awake again, shocked out of her sleep by a voice close to her ear. "He's here!" whispered Ella. "Amy! Wake up! He's here!"

"Who?" Amy cried, and, with pounding heart,

sat up. Her pillow was on the floor, and for a moment she couldn't remember where she was. "Who?" she cried. "Who's here? Who is it?"

"Santa Claus," breathed Ella. "Look. See him out there? In the tree?"

Amy turned sleep-glazed eyes to the double windows. Beyond their closed panes and opened drapes there was the familiar tree, its top swaying in the wind. And what was that hidden way back in its topmost branches? It had what appeared to be a face, and this was blurred, but its silvered hair and flowing, silvered beard stood out. With each puff of the wind its beard gave a little wag.

Amy put a hand to her chest. Lips parted, she leaned forward. Her mind traveled backward. She was six years old again and had never seen the fake Santa Claus with the crooked finger in the department store or in Sally's Diner. It was cold outside. It was a once-upon-a-time Christmas. A red paper bell hung from the lighting fixture in the living room, and beneath it stood the dazzling green tree. On the high closet shelves there were stacks of gaily wrapped presents, and from the kitchen there came the delicious scent of spicy, cooking things. The wind gusted, and with each thrust the house trailer rocked a little.

This was a different wind, this warm, rumoring one stirring the branches of the tree just outside

34

the windows. The wind parted the branches to reveal a balled clump of Spanish moss lodged in one of the tree's forks. Clinging to the ball were long, hairlike streamers of the same silver-colored airplant.

Amy took in a breath. Her vision cleared. "That is not," she said, "Santa Claus out there in that tree."

"No," said Ella from her pillow. "He only comes when it's Christmas and it's not Christmas now." She lay serenely, and in a moment Amy snatched her pillow up from the floor, tucked it into place, and fell back on it.

Presently her dreams came again, and in one of them she was a ball player, but not the kind that sweated or got dirty. She was such an expert at hitting the ball that when it was her turn at bat the pitcher trembled and turned pale. He was from Los Angeles and was famous, yet when the game was over it was not his autograph everybody wanted. It was hers.

There was another dream, but the one with the ball pitcher was the longest and best. It made her laugh, and the sound of her laughter woke her. For a second she lay in comfortable silence, reliving the dream and envisioning a better ending to it, one in which somebody holding a lighted torch came bounding to her and slung a gold medal around her neck. He looked like someone she had seen on television or in a movie, she couldn't remember which. He had an important face and what he had to say to her was important.

She couldn't hear what he said, could not even imagine his words, for now in the room there was a real voice. It was Ella's, and was small and wavering. In the brown darkness it searched. "Mama. Mama?"

"Your mama's not here," said Amy. "Be quiet. Go to sleep. Are you asleep?"

"Mama," lisped Ella. "Mama, where are you?"

Amy rearranged her feet so that under the sheet her toes pointed to the ceiling. "I just told you your mama's not here," she said in a stern voice. "So you can shut up and stop making all those silly noises. They're silly and I don't want to listen to them."

"Mama," murmured Ella. She was lying with her face averted and her breath was coming from her in little, short spurts.

Amy raised up and propped herself on an elbow. To test the cadence of Ella's breathing, to find out if it was the sleep kind, she bent over her bedmate. She smelled the warm, sweet breath and felt the warm sweetness of the little body curled in sleep. These smells crept upward, settled over her, engulfed her.

36

There was a sense of struggle, of being pushed against her will toward some sort of guidance that came, wave upon eerie wave. She smelled the faraway sea.

Disturbed and hating the disturbance, she drew back, slid out of bed, and stood with her head tilted and her arms hanging at her sides. After a long, still moment of this, she decided that she wasn't in the least disturbed and climbed back into bed.

With something of the unknown in it, the wind whispered at the windows.

Two

ON THE MORNING of the first day of summer, Amy sat on the patio with Ella. The sky was dark, and the rain blew across Lake Myrtle in long veils. Ella watched and listened. "It whistles," she said.

"It had better stop pretty soon," warned Amy. "Today's the day the yard man is supposed to come, and he can't cut the lawn or clip the bushes if it's raining." On the table before her she had set a portable lamp and a pedestaled hand mirror and with a small brush was applying Vaseline to her lashes and eyebrows. "We're supposed to go to The Cupboard Door for lunch," she said. "If it's still raining we'll have to take Mama's umbrella because we'll have to walk. Dad said he couldn't come after us. We're going to have chicken livers and rice pilaf."

"If I was home," said Ella, "Brad would find me and he'd take me outside with him so we could feel the rain."

"Old Brad likes to stand in the rain?" said Amy. "I think that's funny. Ha. Ha. Brad had better watch that stuff. Old people aren't like regular ones. They need everything warm and dry. They shouldn't stand in the rain."

"Mama said Brad isn't old," said Ella. "When it was his birthday she baked him a cake and put twenty-eight candles on it."

With a finger Amy dipped into the jar of Vaseline, scooped out a gob, and to make them shine applied a coating of the pale oil to her lips. By choice she was not a morning talker and had found that the best way to avoid early morning decisions and opinions was to merely grunt or mumble. She liked the peace of her usual mornings and had trained her brain not to advance any serious ideas or to produce much thought before noon. Yet as she looked now at Ella she was seized

40

by a current of visionary thought. "This Brad," she said. "He hasn't got him a wife and pile of kids somewhere, has he?"

"He never got married," said Ella.

"Wonderful," said Amy, eagerness mounting. "And he's only twenty-eight. That's not old at all, is it?"

"He can tap dance and jump rope," said Ella.

"Wonderful, wonderful," breathed Amy. She thought tap dancing was vulgar and that jumping rope was not far behind it. Once she had watched a movie that had starred a prize fighter who knew how to jump rope. He talked out of the side of his mouth and at the end of the picture show punched the man he was fighting so hard that a doctor had to come. The knocked-out fighter didn't die, but after that he couldn't keep his head from wobbling so the only kind of job he could get was at a newsstand selling magazines and papers.

Fighting, in Amy's mind, was not necessary and neither was knowing how to jump rope or tap dance, but Ella hadn't said anything about Brad being a fighter and if he wanted to tap and jump that was his doings. "I think men who know how to jump rope and tap dance have got class," she said, making a grab for the only compliment she could think of. She knew about having class or not having it from Grandpa and Grandma Harney.

According to them she herself had none and neither did her father, but her mother did. Class is when you are born better than other people, so you can't buy it. You inherit it from your mother and father. If one of them is lowbrow, you can't have it. Mildred didn't have it. Classy people don't play accordions, they play violins. They aren't truck drivers or shrimpers. They don't live in house trailers. They own land.

"I think Brad must have class," said Amy. "Tell me some more about him."

"When he comes to eat supper with us he brings Mama flowers," said Ella. "He doesn't hit anybody or say bad words. He likes to hear Mama play her accordion and sing."

"I think he must be very classy," said Amy.

"He's nice," said Ella.

"Does your mama like him?"

"Yes."

"How much?"

"She likes him."

"Do they kiss?"

"Yes."

"What else do they do?"

Ella played with her fingers. "After supper Mama gets the book and the paper and the pencil and shows Brad how to read and write."

The current running in Amy's brain ground to a stop. "She does what, Ella?"

"Brad can't read," said Ella, "or write either, so Mama's teaching him how. What's the yard man's name? The last time he was here I asked you to tell me but you didn't. What's his name?"

Astonished at this interrupting and unimportant question, Amy felt her face go blank. The yard man was the yard man. Every week he came in his truck, unloaded his riding mower, and shaved the whole yard. His mower made noise, and sometimes he had trouble with it. He wore a wide-brimmed straw hat, and when his work was finished he drank water from the hose. After that he went around to the back porch and collected his pay. In cash, it was always left for him in the same place, in one of the many empty cans being saved for a someday purpose.

Amy had never exchanged more than six words with the yard man. For all she knew his name might just as well have been a number. She did not know what it was.

Annoyed with Ella's question, Amy pushed herself away from the patio table and went to the door leading back into the Blues' living room. It was high-ceilinged and its furnishings were plain. There was a long bookcase standing against the far wall, and this was crammed to its glass doors with books left over from another time, that time when the Blues lived in their house trailer and, on Sunday afternoons, had sat around sucking oranges and reading. The books in the case were the properties of Mildred and Amy's father and mother and, though in retirement now, they were still protected.

Amy's books occupied four shelves in her room. She was not a happy reader, but a willing one. She read because she had a fear of ignorance. From a canny distance she had studied a couple of people who couldn't read or write. In the supermarket they had to ask somebody to help them buy what they needed because not all of the cans and packages had pictures on them, and in the doctor's office the nurse or one of the other waiting patients had to help them fill out their forms.

According to Amy's father and mother, ignorance was a thousand times worse than being poor. A poor person might have a hard time scraping together the money to buy the baby its medicine, but the ignorant person had it harder because he might give the baby the wrong dose and kill it. People paid taxes to help educate those who couldn't read or write so those who couldn't didn't have an excuse. There was no excuse.

Dejected, her ambition for Brad hanging in

shreds, Amy returned to the patio table. The Vaseline on her lashes had melted, and she wiped them with a tissue before applying a fresh coating. "I don't know the yard man's name," she said. "Anyway, that isn't what we were talking about."

"We were talking about Brad," said Ella. She was wearing a pink beanie and from the pocket of her pink dress took a square of bubble gum. Intently she removed its wrapping, shoved it into her mouth, and began work on it.

"That stuff is not good for your teeth," remarked Amy.

Ella continued to pump her jaws. "Brad gave it to me. It was a present. I've got a whole box. I lost it when Grandma Blue put my stuff away but now I've found it again."

"If your teeth fall out and you have to go to the dentist and get false ones don't expect me to go with you," said Amy. "I'll wait here."

Managing her wad of gum, Ella brought it to the front of her mouth and blew a wispy bubble. It collapsed and she sucked it back into her mouth. Her eyes, so innocent, knew a secret that was aching to be confided. It came. "I didn't tell it to anybody else," said said, "but when Mama comes to get me she's going to drive Brad's car and he's coming too. So Grandma and Grandpa Blue can see how he is. So they will like him."

"Your mama had better not bring Brad down here for anything," said Amy. "He wouldn't fit in for more than thirty minutes."

"They're coming and then all three of us are going to go back to North Carolina," said Ella. "We're going to live in Brad's apartment. It's bigger than ours. He painted it. The room I'm going to have is white and it's got flowers and a tree. They aren't real. Brad painted them on."

With every sense in her alert, Amy slid to the edge of her chair and in a tone of moral judgment said, "You and your mama and Brad can't all live together unless your mama and Brad are married."

Ella tackled another gum bubble and again failed. "Mama said you would be my friend."

"I am your friend," said Amy, peering.

"She told me that and she told me you were as sweet as sugar," said Ella.

"I am your friend and I am sweet as sugar," stated Amy.

Ella turned her head to look out through the patio door, watching the weather. "Mama told Grandpa Blue a story. Why I had to come and stay here a while is, Brad and Mama wanted to get married and then they wanted to go somewhere so they could be by themselves. I wasn't supposed to tell anybody. I don't know why I told you."

46

"You told me," said Amy, "because I am your friend."

"Let's us not tell anybody else till they come after me," said Ella.

"We won't tell anybody else till they come after you," declared Amy. She felt the beat of the pulse in her throat and in her excitement actually considered throwing herself to the floor. Life was right again, free again, hers again!

Kwuk. Kwuk. Down on the lakeshore a great blue heron postured and strutted. There came a shifting in the air currents. The clouds drew back and the sky lightened. The rain was over. The sun shone. The yard man put in his appearance.

Watching the mower eat its way across the side lawn, Ella wanted to know what happened to the grass cuttings. "Where do the parts that get cut off go?"

"They go into that bag on the back of the lawn mower and when it gets full they get dumped into trash bags and the yard man puts them someplace for somebody to carry off," answered Amy. The relief in her pushed her to generosity and she asked, "You want a pickle sandwich? I'm going to have one. We can't go for lunch till noon and that's two hours from now."

The mower had cut its way to the far rim of the lawn and was turning. The sound of its motor stopped. The yard man left the machine, walked several feet from it, sat down close to a bush, and then lay down beside it. He pulled his hat down over his face until only his chin was visible and drew his legs up until he lay in a curled position.

Ella had not missed any of this. Her face puckered with anxiety. "Why is he on the ground?"

"Probably he likes it," replied Amy. And said, "Listen, sport, how soon do you think your mama and Brad will come after you?"

Still with her eyes on the yard man, Ella said, "Maybe he's sick. I think we should go out and see about him. Shouldn't we go out and see about him?"

"He's not sick," said Amy. "He does that all the time. Sport, you didn't answer my question. Do you think your mama will come after you pretty soon?"

"He's sick!" cried Ella, springing up. There was a moment at the door when she couldn't locate its latch, and then she was out and racing across the lawn. When she reached the spot where the yard man was lying, she stopped, her hands outstretched. The man pushed his hat back, looked up at Ella, and stood.

Amy turned her back on the scene. "I told you he wasn't sick," she said to no one. "Such a foo-

foo over nothing." In the kitchen she laid out four slices of bread, placing a layer of flat pickles on two, intending to spread the other two with mayonnaise. The mayonnaise jar had not been opened. It was the same brand her mother always bought, but it was not its usual rich color nor did it taste the same. It was white and flavorless.

Amy eyed the jar and its label. The gummy mess in the jar was the same thing as stealing. Those who made things to sell should always make them the same. If they couldn't then they should change their labels or else go to catching rats for a living.

On her way back through the house Amy stopped at the desk in the dining room long enough to collect a ball-point pen, two sheets of writing paper, and an envelope. She intended to write a letter to the makers of the mayonnaise and it would be one they wouldn't forget in a hurry. Whoever opened it and read it would feel like he'd just been whammed in the back with a bull fiddle. His eyes would bug from his head like a pair of balloons.

The patio was once more occupied by Ella. On the table she had spread a little patch of grass cuttings and was playing a game with them, sniffing them, tasting them, fashioning bouquets

49

of the longer blades. The yard man had gone, taking his mower with him. The driveway where he always parked his truck was empty.

Amy placed her writing materials and the jar of mayonnaise on the table. "He was supposed to have cut the whole yard, not just that little piece out there."

"His name is Rudy Parker and he had to go home because he's got a sick headache," reported Ella. And went on to say, "He lives in the gray house on Mulberry Road and he's got two children, one named Zinnia, she's twelve, and one named John Paul, he's four. And he's been married to his wife for fifteen years."

"She ought to carry him to the doctor for his sick headache," commented Amy.

"I don't see how she could carry him. He's too big," said Ella.

"I meant take," said Amy. "Down here we say carry when we mean take. But don't bother remembering that. You aren't going to be here long enough for it to make any difference. You want to help me write a letter?"

"In day-care I learned how to write my name and some other words," said Ella. "My daddy used to write letters. Who is yours going to be to?"

"To whoever made this mayonnaise," said Amy, and gave the jar such a vigorous push that it fell on its side. She righted it and pulled her sheets of writing paper toward her. "The only thing is, I don't know if the boss is a man or a woman so I guess I'll just put Dear Sir or Dear Mrs. There. Now what else do I want to say?"

"Say where you live and say your name," suggested Ella. "Say you like the mayonnaise."

Amy lowered her eyelids to half-mast and gazed at her companion. "No. I'll write my name and where I live but I won't say I like this mayonnaise. I'm going to say it's ruined and whoever did it had better either go where he's looking or look where he's going."

Ella ate a grass blade. "That will not be a nice letter."

"I don't want it nice," argued Amy. "I want it nasty so they'll pay attention."

"If it was my letter," said Ella, "I would write it nice. Nobody likes nasty. They get mad at nasty. My daddy always wrote nasty and they wrote back nasty. One time he wrote nasty to a man and he came to our house and hit my daddy in the face with a pie. It was lemon."

Amy hesitated. She had never been hit in the face with a lemon pie or anything else for that matter, and to think that nasty only brought nasty made sense. It wouldn't hurt to try nice first. If that failed she could then go to nasty.

Having made her decision, Amy set her pen to paper and asked the distant offender to write back and tell her what had happened to her mayonnaise. She wrote that all of her life she had liked to eat it and look at it but now it was not yellow and it was gummy. She asked, "What happened? Did you pull the wrong switch?" At noon, on her way with Ella to The Cupboard Door, she dropped the letter in a sidewalk letter box.

Myrtle Park's noon was vivid and worthy of notice, yet Amy took no notice of it. With Ella in tow, she skimmed along the streets, watching her reflection in the store windows and bestowing upon it her saucy smile. Tucked away in her, the secret of Mildred's marriage to Brad lay in a comfortable and comforting heap. Every once in a while it raised up and grinned.

Three

THE CUPBOARD DOOR employed two women of few words in its stainless kitchen. At work Amy's father and mother wore white uniforms—pants and short-sleeved jackets buttoned to the neck. Their shoes were white and they wore stiff, white caps that hid all but the fringes of their hair.

Amy loved her mother's hair, the magic of its red glint when it was free of its work cap. Her mother had class and it showed in the proud set of her head and in the straightness of her back. To Amy her mother was an attractive mystery, a private person who moved along with others, giving them what they needed of her, but holding back, always holding back that part of her she needed for herself.

What was needed for herself were the lone, night walks on the lakeshore and the quick, lone trips to Georgia. If she needed more than these things she did not speak of them to Amy. Their relationship was affectionate but, when it came to matters that only concerned Amy's mother, it went a skittish way.

Amy had often thought that her mother might be waiting for something: a change to come, a release, a differentness. Something. The thought was a flirt and tested out to nothing. Her mother's kiss was cool and smooth. She cooked good food and had a tolerant ear for Amy's troubles. She was always home when she was supposed to be. Sometimes in the evenings she sewed.

At The Cupboard Door on this day the family table in the kitchen had been set for two. The promised fare of chicken livers and rice pilaf came from the stove on plain plates, and Amy and Ella were asked to sit and eat.

The phone in the front room of the shop rang and rang again. The bell on the admission's door tinkled. Two clubwomen held a bartering session with Amy's parents. Dignitaries were coming to Myrtle Park. There would be a luncheon for them and should they be served something exotic? What was the cost of the exotic? And what did it include?

At the table in the kitchen Amy addressed herself to the rich food on her plate. Eating to her was a serious and unleisurely affair. She was accustomed to these every-so-often treat lunches that had to be consumed quickly and efficiently. The Cupboard Door was a business, not a place for sitting and dawdling.

"You had better eat," Amy advised Ella. "They're taking care of business and that's where all our money comes from for everything so don't wait for them to come on back here. Eat and then we'll go somewhere else."

"Where?" asked Ella. "Where will we go?"

"To the animal fair," answered Amy, "to watch the old baboon by the light of the moon combing his auburn hair." And laughed. "Or else we'll watch the giraffe sneeze and fall on his knees," she said, and laughed again. It was a time to cut up and say silly things. Brad and Mildred were married, and in North Carolina there waited a room for the little sport.

Ella bent upon Amy a sober regard. "It's not

time for the moon and anyway I don't want to go the animal fair, please."

"I'm glad to hear that," confessed Amy, "because there isn't one. I just made it up. Listen, are you going to eat your livers? They're getting cold."

"Please," said Ella. "Please. I ate one and it was good. But please, I want to take the rest to Rudy. Could we go to see Rudy and take him my chicken livers?"

"You want to take our yard man your chicken livers?" Amy said in a tone of slow discovery. "Well, I will be mortally cooked. Listen, sport, we can't do that."

"Why?" asked Ella.

"Because we can't. See," Amy said. "Rudy's the yard man."

A look of obstinance came over Ella's face. "He's sick. He's got a headache and my chicken livers would help him feel better."

"He doesn't want them," reasoned Amy. "He doesn't need them. Besides, I don't know where he lives."

"In the gray house on Mulberry Road," said Ella. "Please, could I have a piece of paper to put my livers in and could we go then?"

Amy felt the beginning of tension at the back of her neck and forced herself to relax. There was the whole afternoon ahead and nothing to fill it. The walk out to Mulberry Road and back would help it pass. She needn't go into Rudy's house. She would only go as far as his front porch and wait for Ella to go in, deliver the chicken livers, and come back out. Rudy's porch would have a washing machine on it full of clothes that needed washing, and his lazy wife would be there, all whiney and gripey. His dirty kids would be there. Their hair would be hanging in their eyes, but they had never been told it shouldn't so they thought it was natural and never bothered much with it.

To show her how lucky she was, Amy's grandfather had once driven her out to that section of town that contained Mulberry Road, but they had not entered the road. That had not been necessary. Her grandfather knew all about how people like those living on Mulberry Road lived—worse than people who lived in house trailers did. They lived and they died and that was the whole of their story and, but for him, her grandfather, that would be Amy's whole story and her father's too.

On their way out of The Cupboard Door Amy and Ella received the disinterested glances of the two clubwomen and a moment of attention from Amy's mother. Amy held the bundled chicken livers behind her back and said that she and Ella didn't have anything planned for their afternoon except a walk. Her mother said that they should watch where they walked and for them to be good. She turned back to the clubwomen and the question of their exotic luncheon.

In the street the trees gathered their one o'clock shade, and Amy and Ella headed for Mulberry Road. Ella said she couldn't feel how hot it was.

"That's because you're from North Carolina so your blood is thicker than mine," said Amy, breathing the scorched air. "And now it won't have a chance to get thin because your mama and Brad are coming after you. We can't stay long at Rudy's house," she cautioned. "I'll wait for you on his porch and you go in and come right back out. If Rudy's wife wants to give you something to drink don't take it. Tell her you're not thirsty."

"I'm thirsty now," said Ella.

"You drink anything at Rudy's house and it might make you sorry and sick both," said Amy. Since Ella was her responsibility the mild warning was a duty. She swung the bag containing the chicken livers and pursed her mouth, accomplishing a breezy wind sound. "We go this way," she said, directing a course that led away from the town proper.

In the generous distance a lake, smaller than

Lake Myrtle, showed its sparkle and color. There were patchwork fields. The sidewalk ended and ahead lay a stretch of sandy road graced by a single house boasting a weather vane.

Just beyond the road's curve Rudy's house rose, gray and isolated. Sure enough, it was gray, but a respectable gray accented by black outside shutters and the green of growing things pushing out in all directions. In her eagerness to reach the place Ella snatched the bag of livers from Amy's hand and sped ahead.

With all of her former beliefs concerning Rudy and how he lived at a loss, Amy came to the house and saw that its clean, shaded porch was occupied by trellised vines and a long porch swing.

In the swing lay Rudy, no longer in his yard man's clothes. His head was bare and he wore a soft white shirt and soft white trousers. A slender woman with a pleasant mouth and expression hovered over him, cooing, lifting his head to straighten his pillow, to rub the back of his neck, to smooth his hair. She was barefoot, and Amy realized that she was Rudy's wife and, in the same instant, realized that it had been a long time since last she had seen her mother make a fuss over her father. A long, long time since last she had seen that.

Rudy and his wife greeted Ella and Amy as if

they were a couple of special delivery presents. Rudy sat up, opened the bag of livers, ate a couple, and said that the taste of chicken livers always did do something good to his spirit.

Mrs. Rudy wiped his mouth and fingers with a piece of paper toweling fished from her dress pocket and said, "To think that you children would walk all the way from town to bring my husband this caring little gift. Now that does something to my spirit."

"It was Ella's idea," said Amy, yielding to a moment of honesty. "She's my responsibility so it's my job to keep her entertained." And said, "We didn't have anything else to do this afternoon." To her the fact that a walk to Rudy's house was a way to help kill an afternoon seemed a compliment, and it took her a moment to understand Mrs. Rudy's ghost smile. Subdued, she sat beside Ella on the top porch step wondering how long it would be before they could make a polite getaway.

Ella, Rudy, and Mrs. Rudy found things to talk about. Rudy said he believed the livers were helping his headache and told about how, in the evenings, the owls that lived around the place called from their tree hollows.

Mrs. Rudy wanted to know what relation Ella and Amy were to each other, and Ella clapped a hand to her forehead. "She's my aunt but I shouldn't call her that because if I did everybody would think it was funny and they'd laugh."

Far out, where rows of green marched across a piece of farmland, a small boy and a tall girl moved back and forth, bobbing. "That's Zinnia and John Paul," explained Mrs. Rudy. "They're picking our peas."

"I hope," said Rudy, "they'll remember to leave some for the rabbits."

"We always plant a couple of rows for the wild rabbits," said Mrs. Rudy. "Of course they don't know which is which and sometimes get into ours, but we don't squabble over what's theirs and what's ours."

"Boss," said Rudy, "I think our company would like a glass of our good water."

Amy opened her mouth and closed it. When the water was served, she avoided looking at Ella and drank hers down quickly. She opened her mouth again intending to say that it was time that she and Ella got going, but Zinnia and John Paul were coming from the field and Mrs. Rudy left the porch to go out and meet them. They bore a basket filled to its rim with their harvest, and Mrs. Rudy took it from them and brought it to the porch.

John Paul bounced on the balls of his feet and

carried a face full of dreams. Zinnia had thick eyelashes the color of toast and a full suit of toast-colored hair caught up and held back from her face with a barrette. They acknowledged introduction to Amy and Ella with friendly murmurs and an open, friendly searching of their eyes, went into the house and returned, carrying two kitchen pots, seated themselves at the basket, and began shelling the peas, opening the pods and spilling their contents into the pots.

From the swing Rudy said, "What about the rabbits, Zinnia?"

"They were back last night," answered Zinnia, "and finished off their row of parsley and lettuce, but they must be saving their peas for last."

"I love the rabbits," said John Paul.

"You love everything," said Zinnia.

John Paul lifted one of the pea pods to his nose and rolled his patent-leather eyes. "And black-eyed peas. I love black-eyed peas."

"No you don't," disputed Zinnia. "You like them."

"Oh, let him love what he wants," said Mrs. Rudy. "If he loves black-eyed peas, that's his business. If you only like them, that's yours."

"I love the way the grass smells when it's cut," said Ella. "Tomorrow when Mr. Rudy comes back to finish Grandpa Blue's yard, he's going to bring me some paint and a brush and I'm going to make surprises for everybody."

"And Arthur," said John Paul, looking around. "I love Arthur. Where is Arthur?"

"He's out there by the mailbox waiting to see if the mailman is going to bring him a letter today," answered Rudy. The sun had begun to seep through the vines above his head, and he said he thought he'd go inside to rest. Mrs. Rudy asked to be excused and went with him.

Amy stood and, expecting to see a boy or a man, looked out to the Parkers' roadside mailbox. Beside its post crouched a black dog with white ears.

"That's Arthur," said Zinnia. Nimbly she popped a pea into her mouth and ate it with relish. Her eyebrows were two perfect arches. Her skin gleamed.

"Your dog gets letters?" said Amy. "Who from?"

"It's a game," shrieked John Paul. "The letters aren't for Arthur, they're for us, but he doesn't know that."

Turning back to Zinnia, Any was moved to try her hand at a parting compliment. "You have the most beautiful eyelashes and eyebrows. What do you do to them to make them grow like that?"

"Nothing," said Zinnia without conceit, without coyness. "I inherited them from my dad. Notice his sometime, they're the same as mine."

The dog at the mailbox howled mournfully and shook the low bushes at his back. Out on the road again, Amy and Ella passed him and he put a paw over his face and howled again.

Amy wasted a glance on the dog and swung around for a last look at the Parkers' house. Zinnia and John Paul were still busy at their basket. No one had ever told them that they didn't have class. Probably they had never heard of what it meant to have it or not have it, but either way they wouldn't care. Why should they? They had other, more important business. Theirs was the business of picking peas and shelling them, of growing stuff for the wild rabbits and at night of listening to the owls calling from their tree holes.

With a sudden, smoldering dissatisfaction, Amy issued a sharp order to Ella. "Stop puffing like that. You're making me do it and I don't want to."

"I can't help it," puffed Ella. "It's hot and my shoes hurt my feet. I'm going to take them off. Can I take them off?"

"Take them off," said Amy. "But your feet will be hotter with them off than on." Her own feet burned. She watched and waited while Ella lifted first one foot and then the other to peel the socks and shoes from them.

The road lay empty. The short, tough grasses along its shoulders offered a relief from the loose, fiery sand, and Amy and Ella took it. The curve in the road was just ahead, and beyond it the house with the weather vane loomed.

They came abreast of it and Amy, plowing forward, said, "There. It's not much farther now till we get to the sidewalk."

There was no response to this, and she turned to see Ella sitting on the ground. Her face was shock-white and she held her right foot in her right hand. In her left she held a piece of jagged bottle glass. The glass, the heel, and the hands were wet-red. Ella's lips moved and a stricken gasp escaped her. "I didn't see the broke glass and I stepped on it."

Dismayed and enraged at this added and senseless responsibility, Amy stood over her. She wanted to run, to escape. She forced herself to kneel and bend to the injured foot. Its wound appeared wicked, and into the fierce silence she said, "Well, you just had to take your shoes off, didn't you?"

"Yes," admitted Ella in a voice that shook. "My feet were hot."

"Are they cool now?" ranted Amy.

"This one's hurt," said Ella, whispering, "and I can't walk. What should we do?"

"Do?" cried Amy. "What should we do? Why are you asking me that? I'm not a doctor. I don't know what we should do!"

"If we had a rag or something to put around it," said Ella, "maybe it would stop bleeding."

Amy looked up and around. From the little lake in the distance something with pointed wings rose and wheeled away into the sunlight. The house on the far side of the road had a closed look. At its side there hung a line of clothes. The sight of them brought Amy to her feet.

"We need something to tie it up in," faltered Ella, still holding her foot.

"Pesky," grated Amy. "Little pesky. I can't wait for your mama and Brad to come after you." She thought she might see the mail car coming with Arthur's letter and stood in the center of the road, scanning it. The road remained empty. The house on its opposite side had drawn window shades.

Amy pounded first on its back door and then on its front and, when there was no answer, ran around to its side and yanked a long white stocking from the low clothesline there. There was still no sign of the mail car.

66

Bandaging Ella's foot with the stocking, Amy could not resist a lashing comment. "I knew the minute I saw you that you weren't going to be anything but trouble to me and I was right."

"You stole somebody's sock," said Ella. Tears stood in her eyes.

"Well, pooey-dooey," said Amy. "What of it? It's just a sock."

Jerking on its end, she said, "This has to be tight so the blood will stop. It's almost stopped now. What about the cut? Does it still hurt?"

The tears in Ella's eyes spilled. "Oh, Sugar Blue, it does. It hurts."

"Stand up and see if you can walk," directed Amy. "You'll have to walk. I can't carry you and there's nobody out here to help us."

Ella looked away and did not move.

"Ella," ordered Amy, "stand up. You've got to stand up and walk."

"No," said Ella, still with her face averted. "I can't now. I'll do it after a while, but not now. You can go on and leave me here if you want to."

Amy set her teeth. She leaned and slid her arm beneath Ella's shoulder blades. She pulled and the slight weight within the circle of her arm rose and rested against her. She heard Ella's sigh, so soft, so trusting. Swept by a startling sense of change, Amy tried to break away, to move away cleanly, but found that she could not. Within her there was a rush of impressions that throbbed and rumbled and thrashed.

A riffle of wind passed by. Amy drew her breath in, and there was only the sun to see her stiffen and resist—to witness the return of her old, hard confidence.